DEC 2 6 2001

S0-BRW-080

05319118 0

Tales of
Wisdom
& Justice

Also by Pleasant DeSpain

DALY CITY PUBLIC LIBRARY
DALY CITY CALIFORNIA

THE BOOKS OF NINE LIVES

VOLUME THREE

Tales of
Wisdom
& Justice

Pleasant DeSpain

Illustrations by Don Bell

August House Publishers, Inc.
LITTLE ROCK

S

©2001 by Pleasant DeSpain
All rights reserved. This book, or parts thereof, may not be
reproduced or publicly performed in any form without permission.

Published 2001 by August House Publishers, Inc.
P.O. Box 3223, Little Rock, Arkansas, 72203,
501-372-5450.

Printed in the United States of America

10 9 8 7 6 5 4 3 2 1 PB

LIBRARY OF CONGRESS CATALOGING-IN-PUBLICATION DATA
DeSpain, Pleasant.
  Tales of wisdom & justice / Pleasant DeSpain ; illustrations by Don Bell.
    p. cm. — (The books of nine lives ; v. 3)
  Summary: A collection of short folktales from Mexico, Israel, Poland, and
  other places, demonstrating wisdom and justice.
  ISBN 0-87483-646-8 (alk. paper)
  1. Tales. [1. Folklore.] I. Title: Tales of wisdom and justice. II. Bell, Don,
  1935- ill. III. Title.
  PZ8.1.D47 Tal 2001
  398.2—dc21   2001022119

Executive editor: Liz Parkhurst
Project editor & designer: Joy Freeman
Copyeditor: Sue Agnelli
Cover and book illustration: Don Bell

The paper used in this publication meets the minimum requirements
of the American National Standard for Information Sciences—
Permanence of Paper for Printed Library Materials, ANSI Z39.48–1984.

AUGUST HOUSE   PUBLISHERS   LITTLE ROCK

For Eleanor J. Feazell and Edward E. Feazell,
my mother and stepfather.
You are loved and appreciated, always.

Acknowledgments

I'm fortunate to have genuine friends and colleagues without whose help, the first three editions of these tales would not have been possible. Profound thanks to: Leslie Gillian Abel, Ruthmarie Arguello-Sheehan, Merle and Anne Dowd, Edward Edelstein, Rufus Griscom, Robert Guy, Daniel Higgins, Roger Lanphear, Kirk Lyttle, Liz and Ted Parkhurst, Lynn Rubright, Mason Sizemore, Perrin Stifel, Paul Thompson, and T.R. Welch.

I owe allegiance and appreciation to the following for the newest incarnation:

Liz and Ted Parkhurst, Publishers
Don Bell, Illustrator
Joy Freeman, Project Editor

The Books of Nine Lives Series

A good story lives each time it's read and told again. The stories in this series have had many lives over the centuries. My own retellings of the tales in this volume have had several lives in the past twenty plus years, and I'm pleased to witness their new look and feel. Originally published in "Pleasant Journeys," my weekly column in *The Seattle Times,* during 1977–78, they were collected into a two-volume set entitled *Pleasant Journeys, Tales to Tell from Around the World,* in 1979. The books were renamed *Twenty-Two Splendid Tales to Tell From Around the World,* a few years later, and have remained in print for twenty-one years and three editions.

Now, in 2001, the time has come for a new presentation of these timeless, ageless, universal, useful, and so very human tales.

The first three multicultural and thematically based volumes are just the beginning. Volumes four, five, and six will soon follow, and even more volumes are planned for the future, offering additional timeless tales.

I'm profoundly grateful to all the teachers, parents, storytellers and children who have found these tales worthy of sharing. One story always leads to the next. May these lead you to laughter, wisdom, and love. As evolving, planetary, and human beings, we are more alike than we are different, each with a story to tell.

—Pleasant DeSpain
Albany, New York

Contents

Introduction

"There once was a time, long, long ago, when trouble did not exist in the world..." Thus begins the ancient Greek story of Pandora who opened the fabled box to release the evils of sickness, pain, jealousy, lies, and hate upon the earth. Fortunately, she heard the faint cry of Hope, who wanted release as well, in order to bring comfort to those who suffer. Comfort is another way of saying balance or justice. Justice is another way of expressing wisdom.

We know instinctively when an injustice has been committed.

It's human nature to want to correct the imbalance. Thus we call upon our rulers, judges, holy men and women, and often, each other, to make things right once again. Wisdom tales remind us of the value of human experience.

And where there is wisdom, justice usually prevails.

Every country and culture tells tales of wisdom and justice. Here, you'll find stories from Peru and Mongolia, Israel and Mexico. France, Poland, Ireland, Persia, Greece and the United States are represented as well. They help remind us that fairness is necessary if we are to continue to live together as human beings. Enjoy and share these stories!

Pandora's Box

Ancient Greece

There once was a time, long, long ago, when trouble did not exist in the world. Everyone was healthy, happy, and loving. The golden sun shone bright each day, and wild flowers were always in bloom. The earth was a garden of joy.

A young woman named Pandora lived in this garden and she, like all the others, was beautiful and full of laughter. She also, had a quality that was hers alone, and that was curiosity. If Pandora saw a closet, she opened the door to peek inside. If she found a pot on the fire, she lifted the lid to see what was cooking. If she met strangers, she asked many questions to find out as much as possible about them. It seemed as though her curiosity was never satisfied.

One day Pandora came home from playing in the meadow and found a strange and beautiful box sitting near the door.

"Where did this come from?" she asked her husband, whose name was Epimetheus.

"A man carrying a staff with two snakes twisting around it brought the box. He also had little wings on his heels and on his cap," answered Epimetheus.

"That was Mercury, the messenger of the gods, and he must have brought the box for me. I can't wait to see what is inside!"

"No!" exclaimed Epimetheus. "The messenger said that it was not to be opened under any circumstances."

"But how will I know whether or not it's

for me unless I open it?" Pandora asked.

"Forget about the box," said her husband. "Let's go to the vegetable garden and gather our food for this evening's meal."

"No, Epimetheus, you go on alone," sighed Pandora. "I'll just stay here and rest."

As soon as her husband was gone, Pandora began to examine the strange box. It was made of beautifully carved wood. A gold cord with an intricate knot was the only thing that held it shut. She shook the box to see if it rattled, and to her great surprise heard the pleading of tiny voices coming from inside. "Help! Let us out! Please Pandora, untie the knot! Oh hurry, dear Pandora, hurry and open the box!"

She could stand no more. She had to know what was inside. Pandora untied the golden knot and slowly opened the lid to peek inside. Instantly a black cloud filled the room and hundreds of horrible, little insect-like

creatures flew out, shrieking and laughing with cruel voices!

Just then, Epimetheus rushed into the house and was stung by several of the little demons. He screamed and Pandora let the lid fall back in place. But it was too late, for all the troubles on earth had been set free. Sickness, pain, jealousy, hate, lies, and all the other evils flew out of the house and into the world.

Then Pandora heard another little voice coming from inside the box, a voice sweeter than the others. "Please let me out too, Pandora, for I bring help."

She opened the lid once more, and a bright light came from inside the box, chasing the dark cloud away. A tiny creature with golden wings flew up and touched Epimetheus on the shoulder where he had been stung, and the pain that he suffered vanished.

"Who are you?" asked Pandora.

"My name is Hope, and as long as there is trouble in the world, I will be there to comfort all of humankind."

Señor Coyote, the Judge

Mexico

O nce, Señor Rattlesnake was taking his afternoon nap out on the hot sand next to the hole that led down to his cool nest. Suddenly a large stone came rolling down the mountainside and landed on top of him. He wiggled and squirmed and pushed and rolled, but it was no use. He was hopelessly pinned to the ground.

Soon Señor Rabbit hopped by. "Good afternoon, Señor Rattlesnake. I see that you are carrying a heavy rock on your back. Are you planning to build a stone house?"

"Please don't tease me, amigo," said the rattlesnake. "This cruel stone is hurting me and I need your help. Lift it off of me and I will reward you handsomely."

The rabbit had a kind heart and hated to see anyone suffer. Thus he sat on the ground next to the snake and pushed on the stone with his big feet. He pushed hard, and then harder, and even harder! At last the stone shifted and Señor Rattlesnake was free.

"You did well, Señor Rabbit," said the snake. "And now I will reward you."

"Oh, it was nothing," said the tired rabbit. "I don't deserve anything in return."

"Yes-s-s you do," hissed Señor Rattlesnake, and he began to coil.

"What are you doing?" cried the rabbit. "I just saved your life."

"Yes-s-s, I'm going to eat you, and that will be your reward."

Señor Rattlesnake prepared to strike. The

rabbit was too frightened to run and merely stood there, shaking all over.

Just then Señor Coyote walked by. "What is the meaning of this?" he asked.

The snake started to speak and so did the rabbit. Each wanted to tell his side of the story.

"Wait!" said Señor Coyote. "Tell your stories one at a time and I will be the judge. Señor Rabbit, you will be first."

"I found Señor Rattlesnake trapped under the stone. He asked me for help and I pushed it off of him. Then he said he was going to reward me by making me his dinner."

"No, no!" cried the snake. "Señor Rabbit has it all wrong. I crawled under the stone to get out of the hot sun. I could have crawled back out whenever I wanted. I just played a little trick on the rabbit so that I could have him for my dinner."

Señor Coyote looked very serious as he thought about his decision and then asked,

"Do you both agree that Señor Rattlesnake was under the stone?"

They both nodded their heads to say "yes."

"In that case," said the coyote, "I want Señor Rattlesnake to crawl back under the stone so that I can see just how everything was. Then I can judge this difficult case fairly."

Señor Rattlesnake thought quickly and said, "But now that Señor Rabbit has moved the stone, I can no longer crawl under it. You two will have to roll it on me."

Señor Coyote and Señor Rabbit agreed and rolled the heavy stone on top of Señor Rattlesnake.

"Is that just the way you were?" asked the coyote.

"Yes-s-s," hissed the snake. "Now hurry and get this stone off of me!"

"I have a better idea," explained Señor Coyote. "You will stay right where you are, and that will be your reward for being unkind to the one who tried to help you. Good day, Señor Rattlesnake."

The Theft of a Smell

Peru

Once upon a time, there lived a stingy baker in the city of Lima, Peru. Early each morning he mixed flour, milk, eggs, and raisins, and baked his bread, rolls, and cookies. Then he placed the delicious goods in the open window of his shop and sold them to his customers.

The baker was so stingy that he never gave so much as a crumb of his baked goods away, even if it was a stale crumb and the birds were hungry.

The baker's neighbor, however, was a much

different kind of man. He enjoyed a leisurely life and never cared about money or a steady job. In fact, one of his greatest pleasures was smelling the wonderful aromas of the baked goods in the baker's open window. The cool breeze carried the luscious smells to him like a gift each morning. He especially liked the odor of fresh-baked cinnamon rolls.

The selfish baker knew that his neighbor was benefiting from his hard work and he felt that the lazy fellow shouldn't be allowed to have such enjoyment for free. Thus the baker went to his neighbor and said, "You may no longer steal the smell of my baked goods from me. You must pay me five silver coins each month for such a privilege. If not, I'll take you to court."

The neighbor laughed and said that it was a good joke! Then he told all the other neighbors about the baker's special smelling fee, and soon the baker was the laughingstock of the

city. This made him angry enough to speak to a judge.

The judge had a good sense of humor, and after hearing the complaint, ordered both the baker and the neighbor to appear before him the following day. He also ordered the neighbor to bring five silver coins. The baker was quite pleased to hear this and could already feel the weight of the coins in his pocket.

The next day, the courtroom was packed with curious citizens. The judge entered and asked the baker and his neighbor to approach the bench and tell their stories. The baker spoke at length about the beautiful aromas produced by his delicious pastries and how his neighbor had enjoyed them each morning for several years without ever paying so much as a penny for them.

The judge listened patiently to all the baker had to say and then asked the neighbor if he had in fact enjoyed the smells without paying for them. The neighbor replied, "Yes, your honor, it is true."

The judge again spoke to the neighbor, "Take the five silver coins from your pocket and shake them in your hand so that we can hear them clink together."

The man was surprised at such a strange request but did as he was told.

"Did you hear the clinking of your neighbor's silver coins?" the judge asked the baker.

"Yes, your honor," said the baker.

"And does the sound of silver coins clinking together please your ears?"

"Yes," replied the baker.

"This, then, is my decision," said the judge. "The neighbor has enjoyed the smell of baked goods. In return, the baker has enjoyed the sound of silver coins. Case dismissed!"

The Wisdom of Solomon

Israel

Once during the reign of the wise King
Solomon, the Queen of Sheba traveled
from her palace to meet with him. She
brought with her one thousand soldiers,
craftsmen, and attendants, as well as the
most wonderful treasures of her kingdom.

Her artisans had created objects of wonder
and delight such as had never before been
seen! There were birds of gold and silver
that could fly about the room and sing as
beautifully as living birds; a clock made of
wood so rare that it recorded the time of the

past, present, and future; and a carpet woven from the manes of flying horses—a carpet that could fly!

King Solomon looked upon these things and with a calm voice said, "These are works of genius."

The Queen of Sheba clapped her hands and her attendants carried in two vases of flowers and placed them before the King. Then she spoke for all to hear: "O wise and noble Solomon, greatest ruler in all the world, I bring these treasures to you as gifts from my small kingdom. They are to make you smile when your heart grows heavy.

"Now before you rest two vases of flowers which appear to be identical, but only one consists of living flowers. The other is a copy made from gold leaf, precious gems, and brightly colored enamels. Thus I put the following test to the wisest of all living men: which is the true and which is the false?"

Solomon realized that this was no mere game. It was a serious challenge to his reputation as the wisest of kings. If he chose the wrong one, all the world would know of his failure and his glory would be lost.

He gazed upon the wondrous beauty of the flowers, seeking the imperfections that would reveal the false bouquet. The lilies in both vases were perfectly matched, as were the roses and the other blossoms, and each stem wore bright green leaves.

He searched until he discovered a transparent drop of dew on a red rose petal and was about to point his finger to the vase which contained it and say, "These are the flowers grown in nature's garden," but just then he saw an identical dew drop on the same petal in the second vase.

Solomon sat quietly and puzzled over the riddle as everyone in court awaited his answer. Just then, a bee from his garden flew

in through one of the open windows. A guard started after it, but Solomon quickly said, "Do not harm our little friend. Let him alight where he will."

Flying undeterred, the bee soon approached the two vases of flowers. Solomon smiled, realizing that the insect would not be fooled by the artisan's skill, nor by gold, jewels, and false color. Without hesitation, the bee landed on the garden flowers. Solomon raised his hand and pointed to the same bouquet.

The Queen of Sheba bowed before him respectfully, for she too realized that nature is the wisest of all teachers, and even if it is only a bee sent to instruct, it is the wise who listen.

Toads and Diamonds

France

Once long ago, there lived a homely widow and her two daughters. The oldest girl looked just like her mother and was exceptionally ill tempered. The youngest, however, was quite beautiful and had a sweet nature.

The mother favored the oldest daughter and made the youngest do all the housework. One of her daily tasks was to fetch a pail of water from the well in the forest, which was over a mile from the cottage. One day, while she was at the well, a poor old woman came by and begged for a drink.

"Of course you shall have a drink," said the girl. "And I will hold the bucket up for you."

After drinking her fill, the old woman said, "I am a fairy in disguise. I wanted to see if your manners were a match for your beauty, and I'm happy to say that they are indeed. Thus I will give you a rare gift. With every word you speak, a rose or a precious diamond will fall from your pretty mouth."

When the youngest daughter returned from the well, her mother scolded her for being late.

"I am sorry, Mother, for taking so long." And as she spoke, two red roses and three sparkling diamonds came out of her mouth.

"What is the meaning of this?" demanded her mother.

The girl told the story of her encounter with the old woman and the mother said, "It is not you who deserves such a fine gift, it is your sister.

"Dearest," she called, for that is what she always called the elder daughter, "go to the well and draw a bucket of fresh water. When a poor old woman asks for a drink, be sure to give it to her."

"Fetching water is for servants and silly little sisters—it is not for the likes of me!"

"Go this instant," said her mother, "or you will find yourself chopping the firewood as well!"

Thus she went, grumbling all the way. When she reached the well, she saw a beautiful young woman in fine court dress coming out of the woods. This was the same fairy as before who had now taken the form of a princess.

"May I have a drink?" asked the fairy.

"I didn't walk all this way to serve the likes of you," said the unruly girl. "If you want a drink so badly, fetch it yourself!"

"You have but little in the way of manners,"

said the fairy. "My gift for you is that with every word you speak, a snake or a toad will spring from your rude mouth."

The girl ran home and called, "Mother, look at what has happened to me!" And so saying, two black snakes and three green toads leaped out of her mouth.

"It is your wicked sister who has caused all of this!" exclaimed the mother. "And I shall beat her within an inch of her life!"

Upon overhearing the threat, the young girl ran from the house and hid in the deep forest. She knew that she could never return to the cottage again.

Just then, a prince rode by on his way home from hunting, and saw her among the trees. He noted that she looked frightened and asked the reason for her tears.

"It is my mother and sister," she explained. "They have driven me out."

The prince was already taken with her

beauty, and when he saw the roses and diamonds fall from her mouth, he asked her to tell him all that had happened.

Upon hearing the story, he placed her on his horse, and they rode to the palace. Soon after, they were happily married.

The Astrologer and the Forty Thieves

Persia

Once there lived an old astrologer in the great city of Ashkabad, in Persia. His name was Jamal and he was an advisor to the king.

Now it so happened that the king's treasury was robbed of forty chests of precious jewels. The captain of the Guard dispatched his troops and the city was thoroughly searched, but to no avail. Then the king sent for Jamal.

"Tell me, old astrologer, who took my jewels?"

43

Jamal thought for a moment and said, "It was not one man, or even ten, Your Majesty. Rather it was forty—one to carry each chest."

"Excellent," said the king. "Now tell me who they are and where they have hidden the treasure."

"In order to answer you," explained Jamal, "I must have forty days to consult the stars."

"Agreed," said the king, "but if you fail, if the jewels are not returned to my treasury within forty days' time, you will be banished from my court."

Jamal returned home and placed forty figs in a large jar. He planned to take one out each night after his prayers so that he could keep an accurate count of the passing days.

Now, indeed, there were forty thieves, and one of them was an informer at court. When he told his friends that Jamal was able to guess their number, the leader sent one of his men to spy on the astrologer and observe his progress.

He arrived at Jamal's house late that night, just as the old man was finishing his prayers, and listened through a cracked window. Jamal took a fig from the jar and the thief heard him say, "Ah, there is one of the forty."

The thief ran back to the gang and cried, "Jamal has supernatural powers! He can see through walls!"

"Nonsense!" said the leader. "Tomorrow I'll send two of you to keep watch."

The next night two thieves arrived just as Jamal was finishing his prayers. He took a fig from the jar and the scoundrels heard him say, "And now there are two of them."

The frightened thieves ran to tell the others and the following night the leader sent three of his men. The same thing happened that night and the next and the next, until at last, on the fortieth night, all forty thieves were waiting outside Jamal's window.

The astrologer sighed because he hadn't been able to solve the difficult case with his charts and calculations. Then he took the last fig from the jar and said, "The number is complete at last. Now all forty are before me."

The thieves trembled and the leader knocked on Jamal's door. The astrologer was astounded to see forty men file into his house and even more astounded to hear the leader say, "O great and wise man, if you will help to have our lives spared, we will tell you where the king's treasure is hidden."

Jamal went to the king's court the next morning.

"Well, astrologer," said the king, "who has stolen my treasure?"

"Does Your Majesty prefer the thieves or the jewels? The stars above will only tell me one or the other. I cannot give you the answer to both."

"In that case," replied the king, "I choose the treasure."

Jamal consulted his charts as if making a few quick calculations. Then he said, "The treasure will be found in the root cellar of the abandoned estate two miles north of town."

The king was overjoyed to find his jewels and he rewarded Jamal handsomely.

St. Stanislaw and the Wolf

Poland

Once long ago in Poland, when animals still used human speech, a holy man named St. Stanislaw lived in the forest. The saint loved all animals, and he was so compassionate that even the wildest of creatures would come to talk with him. St. Stanislaw listened patiently and always gave good advice, and thus the animals grew to love and trust him.

One morning a large wolf approached the holy man and said, "Good morning, friend."

"And a glorious good morning to you," replied St. Stanislaw.

"I have a problem and I need your advice, kind saint."

"What is the problem, dear wolf?"

"Human meat," said the wolf. "I've eaten every kind of meat available in the land—rabbit, goat, horse, deer, cow, and chicken—but I've never eaten human meat, and the bear says that it is the best of all because it is tender and juicy."

"The bear is only kidding you," said the saint. "Human meat is actually quite tough and dry. You wouldn't like it at all."

"But I must find out for myself, great saint. Please, let me eat a human. I'll only do it once, I promise."

Realizing that the wolf would do it with or without his permission, the saint said, "Very well, you may eat one human, but you must not eat a young or an old person. The only person that you can eat is a blacksmith. Agreed?"

"Agreed!" said the hungry wolf, and he ran through the forest until he came to the road. There he waited for a blacksmith.

Before long, a child on his way to school came by.

"Who are you?" asked the wolf.

"I am a school boy and this is my lunch-box. Do you want an apple?"

"No," said the wolf. "I am waiting for someone else. You go on to school."

Soon an old woman walked by.

The wolf's empty stomach grumbled as he asked, "Who are you?"

"I am an old woman as you can tell by my white hair. I'm going to the village to buy food. If you are still here when I return, I'll give you a nice lump of sugar."

"Then off to the village with you," said the wolf.

Shortly after that, a strong young black-smith wearing a leather apron came along.

The wolf ground his teeth in anticipation and asked, "Who are you?"

"I am the village blacksmith, friend Wolf. Why do you ask?"

"Because St. Stanislaw gave me permission to eat your tender and juicy flesh."

The blacksmith, whose hands and face were covered with soot, said, "I'll taste better if I'm clean. Allow me to wash myself in the river before you eat me."

"Very well," said the wolf, "but hurry, for I am hungry."

The bold young man walked through the trees on his way to the river and found a thick branch shaped like a club lying on the ground. He hid the club in his jacket and then washed his hands and face. Upon returning, he asked if he could dry his wet hands on the wolf's bushy tail.

The wolf agreed and turned around. Immediately the blacksmith grabbed the tail with his strong fist and held tight. Then he pulled the club from his jacket and beat the wolf so hard that he was knocked unconscious. The blacksmith then continued on his journey to town.

When he came to, the poor wolf dragged his bleeding body back to St. Stanislaw's forest hut. The wolf was badly bruised and every muscle ached. When he saw the saint he cried, "You were right as always. Human meat is tough and dry. Never again do I want to taste it."

"Come, my friend," said the gentle saint, "let me clean and bind your wounds."

The Golden Pitcher

Mongolia

There once was a king who feared growing old for he thought that old age was a sign of weakness.

"If I grow old," he thought, "my people will neither respect nor fear me. I must remove all traces of old age from my kingdom!"

Thus he commanded that every old person be either banished from the kingdom or slain.

With tears in their eyes and sorrow upon their hearts, the young people helped their parents and grandparents pack up their belongings in order to leave the country in which they had lived for so long.

The king then took precautions to hide his own signs of age. He dyed his hair to hide the gray and put heavy makeup on his face to cover the wrinkles.

Each day, the youth of the kingdom came to beg the king to be merciful and allow their parents to return. Growing tired of their lamentations, he finally issued a new decree:

"Whoever finds the golden pitcher at the bottom of the lake will be allowed to bring their parents home; but whoever tries and fails will forfeit all his land to the king."

Several adventurous youths and strong-hearted maidens ran to the bank of the deep lake. The clear water shimmered in the sunlight and the golden pitcher could be seen resting on the bottom. It was tall and slender with a curved handle.

Many of the young people dove into the warm water, but all failed to bring the pitcher to the surface. Thus the cruel king grew even more rich with the confiscation of their lands.

At this time there was a young woman named Lillith who loved her old father more than anything in the world. She had hidden him in a mountain cave when the king's order of banishment was issued, and each day she would sneak to the hiding place to bring him food.

One day she said to her father, "I am troubled by the king's pitcher. Why is it that when I look into the water, I can see it clearly, but when anyone dives for it, they return empty-handed?"

Her father thought about this for several minutes and then asked, "Is there a tree on the bank of the lake?"

"Yes Father, a large elm."

"And can the pitcher be seen in the shadow of the tree?"

"Yes," said Lillith, "the shadow of the tree

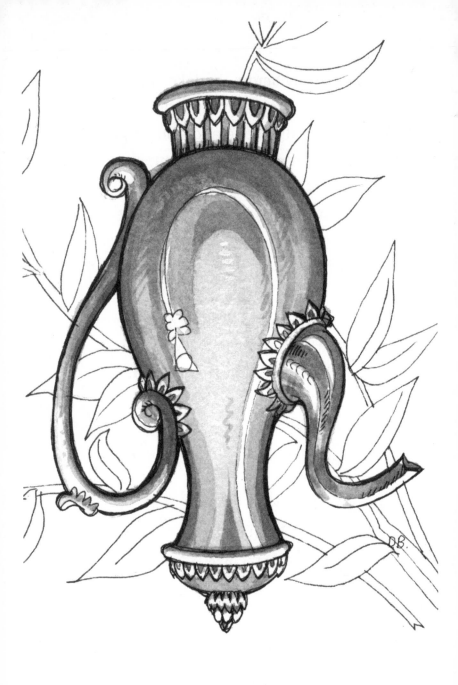

spreads halfway across the lake, and the pitcher can be seen in that shadow."

The old man nodded and said, "You will find the golden pitcher in the branches of the tree. The pitcher that you see in the water is only its reflection."

Lillith ran to the king and said that she would bring the pitcher from the bottom of the lake.

"Very well," said the king. "I will enjoy adding your land to my holdings."

The king ordered his coach and rode with Lillith to the lake. Several of the townspeople ran on ahead so that they could watch the dive.

When all were assembled, Lillith began to climb the spreading elm that grew from the bank. The people thought that she was going to dive from one of the low-hanging branches, but instead she climbed to the very top!

It was there that she found the golden

pitcher with the curved handle. It hung upside down so that in its reflection it seemed to stand right side up on the bottom of the lake. She climbed down from the tree and presented it to the king.

"How did you solve this puzzle?" demanded the king.

"My old father, whom I have hidden from you, figured out the answer."

"Well," said the king, "where fifty youths failed, one old man succeeded. The wisdom that comes with age is valuable after all!"

From that day forth, old age was respected in that kingdom.

Who Will Buy My Horse?

United States

Martin was an honest but poor man
who owned very little in this world.
His only possessions were a strong horse and
an old dog. He loved both of the animals and
often said that he couldn't live without them.

One morning Martin went out to feed the
horse and found that he was gone. He looked
all over the countryside for him, but to no
avail. It seemed as though the horse had
vanished from the face of the earth.

"My good horse must be lost in the
wilderness," said Martin, "with no one to

feed him oats and hay. How I would love to see his brown eyes and hear his happy neigh once more. I wouldn't want to keep him; oh no, I would just like to see that he is all right. In fact, I would sell him for one dollar if only I could see him once again."

Just then, Martin heard a familiar neigh. He looked up and saw something coming towards him in the distance. It looked like a man and a horse. The man was old and gray, and the horse was…was his horse! Martin ran to the horse and hugged him around the neck.

"Where did you find him?" he asked the old man.

"In my field. He was hungry and I fed him. I've been searching for his owner and I suppose that is you."

"I shall always be grateful to you," replied Martin happily.

That night Martin remembered his promise to sell the horse for one dollar if he could but see him again. Since he was an honest man, he knew that he would have to keep his promise. But it was not an easy thing to do, and he thought about it long into the night.

The next morning, he rode the horse to town. The old dog followed behind. When he got to the livery stable he said in a loud voice, "I want to sell my horse, and a fine animal he is!"

"How much do you want for him?" asked one of several men who gathered around.

"One dollar," answered Martin.

"Only one dollar?" someone asked. "Is that all? Just one dollar for this good horse? You must be mad."

"Well," said Martin, "I know that one dollar is a low price, but I also want to sell my old dog. The horse and the dog have been friends for a long time and I don't think they will survive without each other."

Someone in the crowd laughed and asked, "How much for the mutt? He isn't worth a plug nickel."

"Five hundred dollars!" answered Martin. "The horse costs one dollar, but you can't take him without taking the dog, and he costs five hundred dollars. So, who will buy my horse?"

No one bought his horse that day. Martin saddled him up, and with the old dog following behind, headed on home. Halfway there, Martin said aloud, "Well, I tried to sell my horse. Is it my fault that no one was willing to buy him?"

All three lived happily together for the rest of their days.

The Magic Purse

Ireland

Once a young Irishman named Mike O'Hara spied a small man all dressed in green, sitting in the shade of a large toadstool at the edge of the forest. Mike immediately recognized the man as a leprechaun. He had always hoped to catch one because he knew that leprechauns carry a magic purse with a single shilling inside. Each time the shilling is removed another one appears, and thus the purse is never empty.

Now Mike was a lazy sort of man who hated to work, and he thought that his dream of a rich and easy life was about to come true. He crept up to the wee man as quietly as a mouse, grabbed him about the waist, and held him tight.

"Now I've got you, my little friend, and you had better give me your magic purse, or you'll not live to see the sun rise in the morning sky."

"But I'm no leprechaun and I have no purse!" cried the little man.

"Your purse or your life," replied Mike, "and I'll give you but one minute more to decide."

The leprechaun, for that indeed was what he was, reluctantly reached inside his green jacket and pulled out a beautiful purse made of red silk. Then he carefully opened it to show Mike the single shilling inside.

Mike grabbed the purse and set the leprechaun on the ground. The wee man laughed once and then vanished.

Mike was as pleased as he could be with his newfound purse, and as soon as he got back to town, he went to the inn and ordered drinks for everyone.

"Where's your money, Mike O'Hara?" asked Mrs. McCarthy, the owner of the inn. She was suspicious because it was a well-known fact that Mike was always broke.

"Right here in me pocket," said Mike. "I'm a rich man now, and never again will I have to work. Come lads, let's quench our thirst with some good Irish whiskey!"

They drank until the bottle was dry and then Mike called for a grand feast for himself and all of his friends.

"Not until you pay me in cash for the whiskey already gone," said Mrs. McCarthy.

"Right you are," said Mike, and he took the silk purse from his pocket and told them all about his encounter with the leprechaun. "And," he concluded, "every time I take a shilling out of the magic purse, another one appears. Watch."

And hey presto! He pulled the shilling out and...the next shilling failed to appear. The purse was empty!

(It is not as well known, you see, that leprechauns carry two silk purses—one magic and one ordinary—in case they get caught.)

Mike turned red with anger and embarrassment when he realized that he had been tricked. And to make matters worse, he had but one shilling with which to pay for an expensive bottle of whiskey.

"Tell us again about your leprechaun!" laughed the other men.

Mrs. McCarthy called for a policeman and had Mike arrested. When Mike appeared in court, he told the judge that he had been tricked by the leprechaun, and pleaded for mercy.

The judge frowned and said, "I will believe your story only if you produce the leprechaun and he verifies it. Otherwise, thirty days of hard labor!"

Mike O'Hara did his time, and never again did he try to catch a leprechaun.

Notes

The stories in this collection are my retellings of tales from throughout the world. They have come to me from written and oral sources and result from thirty years of my telling them aloud.

All of these tales were previously included in my two-volume set entitled *Pleasant Journeys: Tales to Tell from Around the World* (Mercer Island, WA: The Writing Works, 1979), and later renamed *Twenty-Two Splendid Tales to Tell From Around the World,* (Little Rock: August House, 1990).

Motifs given are from *The Storyteller's Sourcebook: A Subject, Title and Motif Index to Folklore Collections for Children* by Margaret Read MacDonald (Detroit: Neal-Schuman/Gale, 1982).

Pandora's Box — Ancient Greece

Motif C321. If Pandora is blamed for setting free the evils of this world, she also deserves credit for releasing the balancing power of hope. Some, and perhaps more authentic, tellings of this myth end without the release of hope. I couldn't tell it that way.

For other versions, see *Favorite Stories Old and New* by Sidonie M. Gruenberg (Garden City, NY: Doubleday, 1942, 1955), pp. 413–14.

Also, *Pandora's Box* by Lisl Weil (New York: Antheneum, 1986).

Señor Coyote, the Judge—Mexico

Motif J1172.3. This tale appeals to children's innate sense of fair play. Señor Rattlesnake's sense of superiority is fun to play.

For other variants, see *The Buried Treasure and Other Picture Tales* by Eulalie Steinmetz Ross (Philadelphia: Lippincott, 1958), pp. 89–94; and *The Favorite Uncle Remus* by Joel Chandler Harris (Boston: Houghton Mifflin, 1948), pp. 182–86.

The Theft of a Smell—Peru

Motif J1172.2.0.1. The day I actually brought a dozen fresh-baked cinnamon rolls and a handful of quarters to the telling was the most successful of all.

I first discovered this story in *Folktales of Latin America* by Shirlee Newman (Indianapolis: Bobbs-Merrill, 1962), pp. 19–26. See also, *A Kingdom Lost For a Drop of Honey and Other Burmese Folktales* by Maung Hitin-Aung and Helen G. Trager (New York: Parents, 1968), pp. 15–17.

The Wisdom of Solomon—Israel

Motif H540.2.1. I first heard this beautiful story as

a child in Bible class. I often tell it in corporate settings when problem solving becomes the issue.

See *More Once Upon a Time Stories* by Rose Dobbs (New York: Random, 1961), pp. 19–23. *Favorite Stories Old and New* by Sidonie M. Gruenberg (Garden City, NY: Doubleday, 1942, 1955), pp. 357–59.

Toads and Diamonds—France

Motif Q2.1.1. The Cinderella story has more variations than any other fairy tale in existence. Young listeners particularly enjoy the revenge on the sister in this telling.

My initial encounter with this variant was in *The Blue Fairy Book* by Andrew Lang (New York: Longmans, Green, 1919), pp. 295–98.

See also *Candle-Light Stories* by Veronica S. Hutchinson (New York: Minton, Balch, 1927), pp. 93–100.

The Astrologer and the Forty Thieves—Persia

Motif N611.5. A story taken from the Arabian Nights cycle, I first heard it in my sixth grade class. My teacher explained that long ago, in ancient Persia, the term "astrologer" and "astronomer" were interchangeable. I particularly like the astrologer's generous treatment of the thieves.

For other variants see *The Young Oxford Book of Folk Tales* by Kevin Crossley-Holland (Oxford: Oxford

University Press, 1998), pp. 57–61. His version is from *The Blue Fairy Book* by Andrew Lang (New York: Longmans, Green, 1919), pp. 248–58.

See also *The Elephant's Bathtub: Wonder Tales From the Far East* by Francis Carpenter (Garden City, NY: Doubleday, 1962), pp. 49–57.

St. Stanislaw and the Wolf—Poland

Motif B279.1.1. Few stories of saints contain both humor and violence. Though hard on the wolf, I've found the lesson taught easy on the listeners' ears.

I discovered it in *Legends of the United Nations* by Francis Frost (New York: Whittlesey House, 1943), pp. 44–49.

Another variant is found in *Just One More* by Jeanne B. Hardendorff (Philadelphia: Lippincott, 1969), pp. 110–15.

The Golden Pitcher—Mongolia

Motif J151.1.5 As I grow older, and I hope, wiser, I find delight in a tale in which one old man succeeds where fifty youths have failed. A story for all ages, I initially heard it while attending a business conference in Seattle in 1975.

Two variants are found in *Eurasian Folk and Fairy Tales* by I.F. Bulatkin (New York: Criterion, 1965), pp. 22–26; and *The Kaha Bird: Tales From the Steppes of*

Central Asia by Mirra Ginsburg (New York: Crown, 1971), pp. 13–20.

Who Will Buy My Horse?—United States

Motif K182. One of my favorite tales to tell for all ages, it touches the heart and produces a good laugh. It's derived from the Norwegian version in which an ox is offered for five pennies if bought along with a cock for five florins.

See *True and Untrue and other Norse Tales* by Sigrid Undset (New York: Knopf, 1945), pp. 202–8.

For an Iranian version see *Once the Mullah: Persian Folk Tales* by Alice Geer Kelsey (New York: McKay, 1954), pp. 54–60.

The Magic Purse—Ireland

Motif D1451. It's fun to add an Irish lilt to the telling. In order to do Mike O'Hara justice, create a loud vocal, and large physical, characterization.

Other inexhaustible purse tales are found in *The Rose Fairy Book* by Andrew Lang (New York: McKay, 1948), pp. 34-43; and *The Sea of Gold, and Other Tales from Japan* by Yoshiko Uchida (New York: Scribners, 1965), pp. 42-54.

Other Books by Pleasant DeSpain

The Dancing Turtle
A Folktale from Brazil
illustrated by David Boston
Hardback Picture Book $15.95 / ISBN 0-87483-502-X

Strongheart Jack & the Beanstalk
illustrated by Joe Shlichta
Hardback Picture Book $15.95 / ISBN 0-87483-414-7

Eleven Nature Tales
A Multicultural Journey
Hardback $14.95 / ISBN 0-87483-447-3
Paperback $4.50 / ISBN 0-87483-458-9

Sweet Land of Story –
Thirty-Six American Tales to Tell
Hardback $19.95 / ISBN 0-87483-569-0
Paperback $12.95 / ISBN 0-87483-600-X

The Emerald Lizard
*Fifteen Latin American Tales
to Tell in English & Spanish*
Hardback $21.95 / ISBN 0-87483-551-8
Paperback $11.95 / ISBN 0-87483-552-6

Tales to Tell from Around the World
Vol. I Audiocassette $12.00 / ISBN 0-87483-417-1
Vol. II Audiocassette $12.00 / ISBN 0-87483-418-X

August House Publishers, Inc.
P.O. Box 3223 • Little Rock, Arkansas 72203
1-800-284-8784 • www.augusthouse.com

Other Books from August House Publishers

———————

Sitting Down to Eat
Bill Harley; illustrated by Kitty Harvill
Hardback Picture Book $15.95 / ISBN 0-87483-460-0
Paperback Picture Book $6.95 / ISBN 0-87483-603-4

Stone Soup
Heather Forest; illustrated by Susan Gaber
Hardback Picture Book $15.95 / ISBN 0-87483-498-8
Paperback Picture Book $6.95 / ISBN 0-87483-602-6

How and Why Stories
World Tales Kids Can Read & Tell
Martha Hamilton & Mitch Weiss
Hardback $21.95 / ISBN 0-87483-562-3
Paperback $12.95 / ISBN 0-87483-561-5
Audiocassette $12.00 / ISBN 0-87483-594-1
Compact Disc $16.95 / ISBN 0-87483-596-8

Noodlehead Stories
World Tales Kids Can Read & Tell
Martha Hamilton & Mitch Weiss
Hardback $ 21.95 / ISBN 0-87483-584-4
Paperback $12.95 / ISBN 0-87483-585-2

Favorite Scary Stories of American Children
Richard & Judy Dockrey Young
Paperback $4.95 / ISBN 0-87483-563-1
Audiocassette (for grades K-3) $12.00 / ISBN 0-87483-148-2
Audiocassette (for grades 4-6)$12.00 / ISBN 0-87483-175-X

———————

August House Publishers, Inc.
P.O. Box 3223 • Little Rock, Arkansas 72203
1-800-284-8784 • www.augusthouse.com